Judge & Jury: A Short Story Collection

Law is a pinnacle of human society. The phrase 'Be you ever so high the law is above you' inspires us all to believe that before it all are treated equally. But in the imposing wood panelled courts, in front of the beady eyes of wig decked judge, delivering justice tempered with mercy, our vision twists and falls prey to the mind.

For Charles Dickens his story mixes deliberations of the jury with a supernatural varnish. Bram Stoker conjures up life in a house previously owned by a distinctly malevolent judge. For John Galsworthy the pursuit is rather gentler but still unsettling. A juryman must help decide whether an attempted suicide is punished..... Perhaps in our lives we all become both judge and juror.

This book can also be downloaded as an audiobook at Amzon, iTunes and other fine digital stores.

Index of Contents

The Trial For Murder by Charles Dickens

I have always noticed a prevalent want of courage, even among persons of superior intelligence and culture, as to imparting their own psychological experiences when those have been of a strange sort. Almost all men are afraid that what they could relate in such wise would find no parallel or response in a listener's internal life, and might be suspected or laughed at. A truthful traveller, who should have seen some extraordinary creature in the likeness of a sea-serpent, would have no fear of mentioning it; but the same traveller, having had some singular presentiment, impulse, vagary of thought, vision (so-called), dream, or other remarkable mental impression, would hesitate considerably before he would own to it. To this reticence I attribute much of the obscurity in which such subjects are involved. We do not habitually communicate our experiences of these subjective things as we do our experiences of objective creation. The consequence is, that the general stock of experience in this regard appears exceptional, and really is so, in respect of being miserably imperfect.

In what I am going to relate, I have no intention of setting up, opposing, or supporting, any theory whatever. I know the history of the Bookseller of Berlin, I have studied the case of the wife of a late Astronomer Royal as related by Sir David Brewster, and I have followed the minutest details of a much more remarkable case of Spectral Illusion occurring within my private circle of friends. It may be necessary to state as to this last, that the sufferer (a lady) was in no degree, however distant, related to me. A mistaken assumption on that head might suggest an explanation of a part of my own case, but only a part, which would be wholly without foundation. It cannot be referred to my inheritance of any developed peculiarity, nor had I ever before any at all similar experience, nor have I ever had any at all similar experience since.

It does not signify how many years ago, or how few, a certain murder was committed in England, which attracted great attention. We hear more than enough of murderers as they rise in succession to their atrocious eminence, and I would bury the memory of this particular brute, if I could, as his body was buried, in Newgate Jail. I purposely abstain from giving any direct clue to the criminal's individuality.

When the murder was first discovered, no suspicion fell, or I ought rather to say, for I cannot be too precise in my facts, it was nowhere publicly hinted that any suspicion fell on the man who was afterwards brought to trial. As no reference was at that time made to him in the newspapers, it is obviously impossible that any description of him can at that time have been given in the newspapers. It is essential that this fact be remembered.

Unfolding at breakfast my morning paper, containing the account of that first discovery, I found it to be deeply interesting, and I read it with close attention. I read it twice, if not three times. The discovery had been made in a bedroom, and, when I laid down the paper, I was aware of a flash, rush, flow, I do not know what to call it, no word I can find is satisfactorily descriptive, in which I seemed to see that bedroom passing through my room, like a picture impossibly painted on a running river. Though almost instantaneous in its passing, it was perfectly clear; so clear that I distinctly, and with a sense of relief, observed the absence of the dead body from the bed.

It was in no romantic place that I had this curious sensation, but in chambers in Piccadilly, very near to the corner of St. James's Street. It was entirely new to me. I was in my easy-chair at the moment, and the sensation was accompanied with a peculiar shiver which started the chair from its position. (But it is to be noted that the chair ran easily on castors.) I went to one of the windows (there are two in the room, and the room is on the second floor) to refresh my eyes with the moving objects down in Piccadilly. It was a bright autumn morning, and the street was sparkling and cheerful. The wind was high. As I looked out, it brought down from the Park a quantity of fallen leaves, which a gust took, and whirled into a spiral pillar. As the pillar fell and the leaves dispersed, I saw two men on the opposite side of the way, going from West to East. They were one behind the other. The foremost man often looked back over his shoulder. The second man followed him, at a distance of some thirty paces, with his right hand menacingly raised. First, the singularity and steadiness of this threatening gesture in so public a thoroughfare attracted my attention; and next, the more remarkable circumstance that nobody heeded it. Both men threaded their way among the other passengers with a smoothness hardly consistent even with the action of walking on a pavement; and no single creature, that I could see, gave them place, touched them, or looked after them. In passing before my windows, they both stared up at me. I saw their two faces very distinctly, and I knew that I could recognise them anywhere. Not that I had consciously noticed anything very remarkable in either face, except that the man who went first had an unusually lowering appearance, and that the face of the man who followed him was of the colour of impure wax.

I am a bachelor, and my valet and his wife constitute my whole establishment. My occupation is in a certain Branch Bank, and I wish that my duties as head of a Department were as light as they are popularly supposed to be. They kept me in town that autumn, when I stood in need of change. I was not ill, but I was not well. My reader is to make the most that can be reasonably made of my feeling jaded, having a depressing sense upon me of a monotonous life, and being "slightly dyspeptic." I am assured by my renowned doctor that my real state of health at that time justifies no stronger description, and I quote his own from his written answer to my request for it.

As the circumstances of the murder, gradually unravelling, took stronger and stronger possession of the public mind, I kept them away from mine by knowing as little about them as was possible in the midst of the universal excitement. But I knew that a verdict of Wilful Murder had been found against the suspected murderer, and that he had been committed to Newgate for trial. I also knew that his trial had been postponed over one Sessions of the Central Criminal Court, on the ground of general prejudice and want of time for the preparation of the defence. I may further have known, but I believe I did not, when, or about when, the Sessions to which his trial stood postponed would come on.

My sitting-room, bedroom, and dressing-room, are all on one floor. With the last there is no communication but through the bedroom. True, there is a door in it, once communicating with the staircase; but a part of the fitting of my bath has been and had then been for some years fixed across it. At the same period, and as a part of the same arrangement, the door had been nailed up and canvased over.

I was standing in my bedroom late one night, giving some directions to my servant before he went to bed. My face was towards the only available door of communication with the dressing-room, and it was closed. My servant's back was towards that door. While I was speaking to him, I saw it open, and a man look in, who very earnestly and mysteriously beckoned to me. That man was the man who had gone second of the two along Piccadilly, and whose face was of the colour of impure wax.

The figure, having beckoned, drew back, and closed the door. With no longer pause than was made by my crossing the bedroom, I opened the dressing-room door, and looked in. I had a lighted candle already in my hand. I felt no inward expectation of seeing the figure in the dressing-room, and I did not see it there.

Conscious that my servant stood amazed, I turned round to him, and said: "Derrick, could you believe that in my cool senses I fancied I saw a" As I there laid my hand upon his breast, with a sudden start he trembled violently, and said, "O Lord, yes, sir! A dead man beckoning!"

Now I do not believe that this John Derrick, my trusty and attached servant for more than twenty years, had any impression whatever of having seen any such figure, until I touched him. The change in him was so startling, when I touched him, that I fully believe he derived his impression in some occult manner from me at that instant.

I bade John Derrick bring some brandy, and I gave him a dram, and was glad to take one myself. Of what had preceded that night's phenomenon, I told him not a single word. Reflecting on it, I was absolutely certain that I had never seen that face before, except on the one occasion in Piccadilly. Comparing its expression when beckoning at the door with its expression when it had stared up at me as I stood at my window, I came to the conclusion that on the first occasion it had sought to fasten itself upon my memory, and that on the second occasion it had made sure of being immediately remembered.

I was not very comfortable that night, though I felt a certainty, difficult to explain, that the figure would not return. At daylight I fell into a heavy sleep, from which I was awakened by John Derrick's coming to my bedside with a paper in his hand.

This paper, it appeared, had been the subject of an altercation at the door between its bearer and my servant. It was a summons to me to serve upon a Jury at the forthcoming Sessions of the Central Criminal Court at the Old Bailey. I had never before been summoned on such a Jury, as John Derrick well knew. He believed, I am not certain at this hour whether with reason or otherwise, that that class of Jurors were customarily chosen on a lower qualification than mine, and he had at first refused to accept the summons. The man who served it had taken the matter very coolly. He had said that my attendance or non-attendance was nothing to him; there the summons was; and I should deal with it at my own peril, and not at his.

For a day or two I was undecided whether to respond to this call, or take no notice of it. I was not conscious of the slightest mysterious bias, influence, or attraction, one way or other. Of that I am as strictly sure as of every other statement that I make here. Ultimately I decided, as a break in the monotony of my life, that I would go.

The appointed morning was a raw morning in the month of November. There was a dense brown fog in Piccadilly, and it became positively black and in the last degree oppressive East of Temple Bar. I found the passages and staircases of the Court-House flaringly lighted with gas, and the Court itself similarly illuminated. I THINK that, until I was conducted by officers into the Old Court and saw its crowded state, I did not know that the Murderer was to be tried that day. I THINK that, until I was so helped into the Old Court with considerable difficulty, I did not know into which of the two Courts sitting my summons would take me. But this must not be received as a positive assertion, for I am not completely satisfied in my mind on either point.

I took my seat in the place appropriated to Jurors in waiting, and I looked about the Court as well as I could through the cloud of fog and breath that was heavy in it. I noticed the black vapour hanging like a murky curtain outside the great windows, and I noticed the stifled sound of wheels on the straw or tan that was littered in the street; also, the hum of the people gathered there, which a shrill whistle, or a louder song or hail than the rest, occasionally pierced. Soon afterwards the Judges, two in number, entered, and took their seats. The buzz in the Court was awfully hushed. The direction was given to put the Murderer to the bar. He appeared there. And in that same instant I recognised in him the first of the two men who had gone down Piccadilly.

If my name had been called then, I doubt if I could have answered to it audibly. But it was called about sixth or eighth in the panel, and I was by that time able to say, "Here!" Now, observe. As I stepped into the box, the prisoner, who had been looking on attentively, but with no sign of concern, became violently agitated, and beckoned to his attorney. The prisoner's wish to challenge me was so manifest, that it occasioned a pause, during which the attorney, with his hand upon the dock, whispered with his client, and shook his head. I afterwards had it from that gentleman, that the prisoner's first affrighted words to him were, "AT ALL HAZARDS, CHALLENGE THAT MAN!" But that, as he would give no reason for it, and admitted that he had not even known my name until he heard it called and I appeared, it was not done.

Both on the ground already explained, that I wish to avoid reviving the unwholesome memory of that Murderer, and also because a detailed account of his long trial is by no means indispensable to my narrative, I shall confine myself closely to such incidents in the ten days and nights during which we, the Jury, were kept together, as directly bear on my own curious personal experience. It is in that, and not in the Murderer, that I seek to interest my reader. It is to that, and not to a page of the Newgate Calendar, that I beg attention.

I was chosen Foreman of the Jury. On the second morning of the trial, after evidence had been taken for two hours (I heard the church clocks strike), happening to cast my eyes over my brother jurymen, I found an inexplicable difficulty in counting them. I counted them several times, yet always with the same difficulty. In short, I made them one too many.

I touched the brother jurymen whose place was next me, and I whispered to him, "Oblige me by counting us." He looked surprised by the request, but turned his head and counted. "Why," says he, suddenly, "we are Thirt—; but no, it's not possible. No. We are twelve."

According to my counting that day, we were always right in detail, but in the gross we were always one too many. There was no appearance, no figure, to account for it; but I had now an inward foreshadowing of the figure that was surely coming.

The Jury were housed at the London Tavern. We all slept in one large room on separate tables, and we were constantly in the charge and under the eye of the officer sworn to hold us in safe-keeping. I see no reason for suppressing the real name of that officer. He was intelligent, highly polite, and obliging, and (I was glad to hear) much respected in the City. He had an agreeable presence, good eyes, enviable black whiskers, and a fine sonorous voice. His name was Mr. Harker.

When we turned into our twelve beds at night, Mr. Harker's bed was drawn across the door. On the night of the second day, not being disposed to lie down, and seeing Mr. Harker sitting on his bed, I went and sat beside him, and offered him a pinch of snuff. As Mr. Harker's hand touched mine in taking it from my box, a peculiar shiver crossed him, and he said, "Who is this?"

Following Mr. Harker's eyes, and looking along the room, I saw again the figure I expected, the second of the two men who had gone down Piccadilly. I rose, and advanced a few steps; then stopped, and looked round at Mr. Harker. He was quite unconcerned, laughed, and said in a pleasant way, "I thought for a moment we had a thirteenth juryman, without a bed. But I see it is the moonlight."

Making no revelation to Mr. Harker, but inviting him to take a walk with me to the end of the room, I watched what the figure did. It stood for a few moments by the bedside of each of my eleven brother jurymen, close to the pillow. It always went to the right-hand side of the bed, and always passed out crossing the foot of the next bed. It seemed, from the action of the head, merely to look down pensively at each recumbent figure. It took no notice of me, or of my bed, which was that nearest to Mr. Harker's. It seemed to go out where the moonlight came in, through a high window, as by an aerial flight of stairs.

Next morning at breakfast, it appeared that everybody present had dreamed of the murdered man last night, except myself and Mr. Harker.

I now felt as convinced that the second man who had gone down Piccadilly was the murdered man (so to speak), as if it had been borne into my comprehension by his immediate testimony. But even this took place, and in a manner for which I was not at all prepared.

On the fifth day of the trial, when the case for the prosecution was drawing to a close, a miniature of the murdered man, missing from his bedroom upon the discovery of the deed, and afterwards found in a hiding-place where the Murderer had been seen digging, was put in evidence. Having been identified by the witness under examination, it was handed up to the Bench, and thence handed down to be inspected by the Jury. As an officer in a black gown was making his way with it across to me, the figure of the second man who had gone down Piccadilly impetuously started from the crowd, caught the miniature from the officer, and gave it to me with his own hands, at the same time saying, in a low and hollow tone, before I saw the miniature, which was in a locket, "I WAS YOUNGER THEN, AND MY FACE WAS NOT THEN DRAINED OF BLOOD." It also came between me and the brother juryman to whom I would have given the miniature, and between him and the brother juryman to whom he would have given it, and so passed it on through the whole of our number, and back into my possession. Not one of them, however, detected this.

At table, and generally when we were shut up together in Mr. Harker's custody, we had from the first naturally discussed the day's proceedings a good deal. On that fifth day, the case for the prosecution being closed, and we having that side of the question in a completed shape before us, our discussion was more animated and serious. Among our number was a vestryman, the densest idiot I have ever seen at large, who met the plainest evidence with the most preposterous objections, and who was sided with by two flabby parochial parasites; all the three impanelled from a district so delivered over to Fever that they ought to have been upon their own trial for five hundred Murders. When these mischievous blockheads were at their loudest, which was towards midnight, while some of us were already preparing for bed, I again saw the murdered man. He stood grimly behind them, beckoning to me. On my going towards them, and striking into the conversation, he immediately retired. This was the beginning of a separate series of appearances, confined to that long room in which we were confined. Whenever a knot of my brother jurymen laid their heads together, I saw the head of the murdered man among theirs. Whenever their comparison of notes was going against him, he would solemnly and irresistibly beckon to me.

It will be borne in mind that down to the production of the miniature, on the fifth day of the trial, I had never seen the Appearance in Court. Three changes occurred now that we entered on the case for the defence. Two of them I will mention together, first. The figure was now in Court continually, and it never there addressed itself to me, but always to the person who was speaking at the time. For instance: the throat of the murdered man had been cut straight across. In the opening speech for the defence, it was suggested that the deceased might have cut his own throat. At that very moment, the figure, with its throat in the dreadful condition referred to (this it had concealed before), stood at the speaker's elbow, motioning across and across its windpipe, now with the right hand, now with the left, vigorously suggesting to the speaker himself the impossibility of such a wound having been self-inflicted by either hand. For another instance: a witness to character, a woman, deposed to the prisoner's being the most amiable of mankind. The figure at that instant stood on the floor before her, looking her full in the face, and pointing out the prisoner's evil countenance with an extended arm and an outstretched finger.

The third change now to be added impressed me strongly as the most marked and striking of all. I do not theorise upon it; I accurately state it, and there leave it. Although the Appearance was not itself perceived by those whom it addressed, its coming close to such persons was invariably attended by some trepidation or disturbance on their part. It seemed to me as if it were prevented, by laws to which I was not amenable, from fully revealing itself to others, and yet as if it could invisibly, dumbly, and darkly overshadow their minds. When the leading counsel for the defence suggested that hypothesis of suicide, and the figure stood at the learned gentleman's elbow, frightfully sawing at its severed throat, it is undeniable that the counsel faltered in his speech, lost for a few seconds the thread of his ingenious discourse, wiped his forehead with his handkerchief, and turned extremely pale. When the witness to character was confronted by the Appearance, her eyes most certainly did follow the direction of its pointed finger, and rest in great hesitation and trouble upon the prisoner's face. Two additional illustrations will suffice. On the eighth day of the trial, after the pause which was every day made early in the afternoon for a few minutes' rest and refreshment, I came back into Court with the rest of the Jury some little time before the return of the Judges. Standing up in the box and looking about me, I thought the figure was not there, until, chancing to raise my eyes to the gallery, I saw it bending forward, and leaning over a very decent woman, as if to assure itself whether the Judges had resumed their seats or not. Immediately afterwards that woman screamed, fainted, and was carried out. So with the venerable, sagacious, and patient Judge who conducted the trial. When the case was over, and he settled himself and his papers to sum up, the murdered man, entering by the Judges' door, advanced to his Lordship's desk, and looked eagerly over his shoulder at the pages of his notes which he was turning. A change came over his Lordship's face; his hand stopped; the peculiar shiver, that I knew so well, passed over him; he faltered, "Excuse me, gentlemen, for a few moments. I am somewhat oppressed by the vitiated air;" and did not recover until he had drunk a glass of water.

Through all the monotony of six of those interminable ten days, the same Judges and others on the bench, the same Murderer in the dock, the same lawyers at the table, the same tones of question and answer rising to the roof of the court, the same scratching of the Judge's pen, the same ushers going in and out, the same lights kindled at the same hour when there had been any natural light of day, the same foggy curtain outside the great windows when it was foggy, the same rain pattering and dripping when it was rainy, the same footmarks of turnkeys and prisoner day after day on the same sawdust, the same keys locking and unlocking the same heavy doors, through all the wearisome monotony which made me feel as if I had been Foreman of the Jury for a vast cried of time, and Piccadilly had flourished coevally with Babylon, the murdered man never lost one trace of his distinctness in my eyes, nor was he at any moment less distinct than anybody else. I must not omit, as a matter of fact, that I never once saw the Appearance which I call by the name of the murdered man look at the Murderer. Again and again I wondered, "Why does he not?" But he never did.

Nor did he look at me, after the production of the miniature, until the last closing minutes of the trial arrived. We retired to consider, at seven minutes before ten at night. The idiotic vestryman and his two parochial parasites gave us so much trouble that we twice returned into Court to beg to have certain extracts from the Judge's notes re-read. Nine of us had not the smallest doubt about those passages, neither, I believe, had any one in the Court; the dunder-headed triumvirate, having no idea but obstruction, disputed them for that very reason. At length we prevailed, and finally the Jury returned into Court at ten minutes past twelve.

The murdered man at that time stood directly opposite the Jury-box, on the other side of the Court. As I took my place, his eyes rested on me with great attention; he seemed satisfied, and slowly shook a great gray veil, which he carried on his arm for the first time, over his head and whole form. As I gave in our verdict, "Guilty," the veil collapsed, all was gone, and his place was empty.

The Murderer, being asked by the Judge, according to usage, whether he had anything to say before sentence of Death should be passed upon him, indistinctly muttered something which was described in the leading newspapers of the following day as "a few rambling, incoherent, and half-audible words, in which he was understood to complain that he had not had a fair trial, because the Foreman of the Jury was prepossessed against him." The remarkable declaration that he really made was this: "MY LORD, I KNEW I WAS A DOOMED MAN, WHEN THE FOREMAN OF MY JURY CAME INTO THE BOX. MY LORD, I KNEW HE WOULD NEVER LET ME OFF, BECAUSE, BEFORE I WAS TAKEN, HE SOMEHOW GOT TO MY BEDSIDE IN THE NIGHT, WOKE ME, AND PUT A ROPE ROUND MY NECK."

The Judge's House by Bram Stoker

When the time for his examination drew near Malcolm Malcolmson made up his mind to go somewhere to read by himself. He feared the attractions of the seaside, and also he feared completely rural isolation, for of old he knew its charms, and so he determined to find some unpretentious little town where there would be nothing to distract him. He refrained from asking suggestions from any of his friends, for he argued that each would recommend some place of which he had knowledge, and where he had already acquaintances. As Malcolmson wished to avoid friends he had no wish to encumber himself with the attention of friends' friends and so he determined to look out for a place for himself. He packed a portmanteau with some clothes and all the books he required, and then took ticket for the first name on the local time-table which he did not know.

When at the end of three hours' journey he alighted at Benchurch, he felt satisfied that he had so far obliterated his tracks as to be sure of having a peaceful opportunity of pursuing his studies. He went straight to the one inn which the sleepy little place contained, and put up for the night. Benchurch was a market town, and once in three weeks was crowded to excess, but for the reminder of the twenty-one days it was as attractive as a desert. Malcolmson looked around the day after his arrival to try to find quarters more isolated than even so quiet an inn as "The Good Traveller" afforded. There was only one place which took his fancy, and it certainly satisfied his wildest ideas regarding quiet; in fact, quiet was not the proper word to apply to it—desolation was the only term conveying any suitable idea of its isolation. It was an old, rambling, heavy-built house of the Jacobean style, with heavy gables and windows, unusually small, and set higher than was customary in such houses, and was surrounded with a high brick wall massively built. Indeed, on examination, it looked more like a fortified house than an ordinary dwelling. But all these things pleased Malcolmson. "Here," he thought, "is the very spot I have been looking for, and if I can only get opportunity of using it I shall be happy." His joy was increased when he realized beyond doubt that it was not at present inhabited.

From the post-office he got the name of the agent, who was rarely surprised at the application to rent a part of the old house. Mr. Carnford, the local lawyer and agent, was a genial old gentleman, and frankly confessed his delight at anyone being willing to live in the house.

"To tell you the truth," said he, "I should be only too happy, on behalf of the owners, to let anyone have the house rent free, for a term of years if only to accustom the people here to see it inhabited. It has been so long empty that some kind of absurd prejudice has grown up about it, and this can be best put down by its occupation—if only," he added with a sly glance at Malcolmson, "by a scholar like yourself, who wants its quiet for a time."

Malcolmson thought it needless to ask the agent about the "absurd prejudice"; he knew he would get more information, if he should require it, on that subject from other quarters. He paid his three months' rent, got a receipt, and the name of an old woman who would probably undertake to "do" for him, and came away with the keys in his pocket. He then went to the landlady of the inn, who was a cheerful and most kindly person, and asked her advice as to such stores and provisions as he would be likely to require. She threw up her hands in amazement when he told her where he was going to settle himself.

"Not in the Judge's House!" she said, and grew pale as she spoke. He explained the locality of the house, saying that he did not know its name. When he had finished she answered:

"Aye, sure enough—sure enough the very place! It is the Judge's House sure enough." He asked her to tell him about the place, why so called, and what there was against it. She told him that it was so called locally because it had been many years before—how long she could not say, as she was herself from another part of the country, but she thought it must have been a hundred years or more—the abode of a judge who was held in great terror on account of his harsh sentences and his hostility to prisoners at Assizes. As to what there was against the house she could not tell. She had often asked, but no one could inform her, but there was a general feeling that there was something, and for her own part she would not take all the money in Drinkwater's Bank and stay in the house an hour by herself. Then she apologized to Malcolmson for her disturbing talk.

"It is too bad of me, sir, and you—and a young gentleman, too—if you will pardon me saying it, going to live there all alone. If you were my boy—and you'll excuse me for saying it—you wouldn't sleep there a night, not if I had to go there myself and pull the big alarm bell that's on the roof!" The good creature was so manifestly in earnest, and was so kindly in her intentions, that Malcolmson, although amused, was touched. He told her kindly how much he appreciated her interest in him, and added:

"But, my dear Mrs. Witham, indeed you need not be concerned about me! A man who is reading for the Mathematical Tripos has too much to think of to be disturbed by any of these mysterious 'somethings,' and his work is of too exact and prosaic a kind to allow of his having any order in his mind for mysteries of any kind. Harmonical Progression, Permutations and Combinations, and Elliptic Functions have sufficient mysteries for me!" Mrs. Witham kindly undertook to see after his commissions, and he went himself to look for the old woman who had been recommended to him. When he turned to the Judge's House with her, after an interval of a couple of hours, he found Mrs. Witham herself waiting with several men and boys carrying parcels, and an upholsterer's man with a bed in a cart, for she said, though table and chairs might be all very well, a bed that hadn't been aired for maybe fifty years was not proper for young ones to lie on. She was evidently curious to see the inside of the house, and though manifestly so afraid of the 'somethings' that at the slightest sound she clutched on to Malcolmson, whom she never left for a moment, went over the whole place.

After his examination of the house, Malcolmson decided to take up his abode in the great dining-room, which was big enough to serve for all his requirements, and Mrs. Witham, with the aid of the charwoman, Mrs. Dempster, proceeded to arrange matters. When the hampers were brought in and unpacked, Malcolmson saw that with much kind forethought she had sent from her own kitchen sufficient provisions to last for a few days. Before going she expressed all sorts of kind wishes, and at the door turned and said:

"And perhaps, sir, as the room is big and draughty it might be well to have one of those big screens put round your bed at night—though truth to tell, I would die myself if I were to be so shut in with all kinds of — of 'things,' that put their heads round the sides or over the top, and look on me!" The image which she had called up was too much for her nerves and she fled incontinently.

Mrs. Dempster sniffed in a superior manner as the landlady disappeared, and remarked that for her own part she wasn't afraid of all the bogies in the kingdom.

"I'll tell you what it is, sir," she said, "bogies is all kinds and sorts of things—except bogies! Rats and mice, and beetles and creaky doors, and loose slates, and broken panes, and stiff drawer handles, that stay out when you pull them and then fall down in the middle of the night. Look at the wainscot of the room! It is old—hundreds of years old! Do you think there's no rats and beetles there? And do you imagine, sir, that you won't see none of them? Rats is bogies, I tell you, and bogies is rats, and don't you get to think anything else!"

"Mrs. Dempster," said Malcolmson gravely, making her a polite bow, "you know more than a Senior Wrangler! And let me say that, as a mark of esteem for your indubitable soundness of head and heart, I shall, when I go, give you possession of this house, and let you stay here by yourself for the last two months of my tenancy, for four weeks will serve my purpose."

"Thank you kindly, sir!" she answered, "but I couldn't sleep away from home a night. I am in Greenhow's Charity, and if I slept a night away from my rooms I should lose all I have got to live on. The rules is very strict, and there's too many watching for a vacancy for me to run any risks in the matter. Only for that, sir, I'd gladly come here and attend on you altogether during your stay."

"My good woman," said Malcolmson hastily, "I have come here on a purpose to obtain solitude, and believe me that I am grateful to the late Greenhow for having organized his admirable charity—whatever it is—that I am perforce denied the opportunity of suffering from such a form of temptation! Saint Anthony himself could not be more rigid on the point!"

The old woman laughed harshly. "Ah, you young gentlemen," she said, "you don't fear for nought, and belike you'll get all the solitude you want here." She set to work with her cleaning, and by nightfall, when Malcolmson returned from his walk—he always had one of his books to study as he walked—he found the room swept and tidied, a fire burning on the old hearth, the lamp lit, and the table spread for supper with Mrs. Witham's excellent fare. "This is comfort indeed," he said, and rubbed his hands.

When he had finished his supper, and lifted the tray to the other end of the great oak dining-table, he got out his books again, put fresh wood on the fire, trimmed his lamp, and set himself down to a spell of real hard work. He went on without a pause till about eleven o'clock, when he knocked off for a bit to fix his fire and lamp, and to make himself a cup of tea. He had always been a tea-drinker, and during his college life had sat late at work and had taken tea late. The rest was a great luxury to him, and he enjoyed it with a sense of delicious voluptuous ease. The renewed fire leaped and sparkled, and threw quaint shadows through the great old room, and as he sipped his hot tea he revelled in the sense of isolation from his kind. Then it was that he began to notice for the first time what a noise the rats were making.

"Surely," he thought, "they cannot have been at it all the time I was reading. Had they been, I must have noticed it!" Presently, when the noise increased, he satisfied himself that it was really new. It was evident that at first the rats had been frightened at the presence of a stranger, and the light of fire and lamp, but that as the time went on they had grown bolder and were now disporting themselves as was their wont.

How busy they were—and hark to the strange noises! Up and down the old wainscot, over the ceiling and under the floor they raced, and gnawed, and scratched! Malcolmson smiled to himself as he recalled to mind the saying of Mrs. Dempster, "Bogies is rats, and rats is bogies!" The tea began to have its effect of intellectual and nervous stimulus, he saw with joy another long spell of work to be done before the night was past, and in the sense of security which it gave him, he allowed himself the luxury of a good look round the room. He took his lamp in one hand, and went all round, wondering that so quaint and beautiful an old house had been so long neglected. The carving of the oak on the panels of the wainscot was fine, and on and round the doors and windows it was beautiful and of rare merit. There were some old pictures on the walls, but they were coated so thick with dust and dirt that he could not distinguish any detail of them, though he held his lamp as high as he could over his head. Here and there as he went round he saw some crack or hole blocked for a moment by the face of a rat with its bright eyes glittering in the light, but in an instant it was gone, and a squeak and a scamper followed. The thing that most struck him, however, was the rope of the great alarm bell on the roof, which hung down in a corner of the room on the right-hand side of the fireplace. He pulled up close to the hearth a great high-backed carved oak chair, and sat down to his last cup of tea. When this was done he made up the fire, and went back to his work, sitting at the corner of the table, having the fire to his left. For a little while the rats disturbed him somewhat with their perpetual scampering, but he got accustomed to the noise as one does to the ticking of the clock or to the roar of moving water, and he became so immersed in his work that everything in the world, except the problem which he was trying to solve, passed away from him.

He suddenly looked up, his problem was still unsolved, and there was in the air that sense of the hour before the dawn, which is so dread to doubtful life. The noise of the rats had ceased. Indeed it seemed to him that it must have ceased but lately and that it was the sudden cessation which had disturbed him. The fire had fallen low, but still it threw out a deep red glow. As he looked he started in spite of his sang froid.

There, on the great high-backed carved oak chair by the right side of the fire-place sat an enormous rat, steadily glaring at him with baleful eyes. He made a motion to it as though to hunt it away, but it did not stir. Then he made the motion of throwing something. Still it did not stir, but showed its great white teeth angrily, and its cruel eyes shone in the lamplight with an added vindictiveness.

Malcolmson felt amazed, and seizing the poker from the hearth ran at it to kill it. Before, however, he could strike it the rat, with a squeak that sounded like the concentration of hate, jumped upon the floor, and, running up the rope of the alarm bell, disappeared in the darkness beyond the range of the green-shaded lamp. Instantly, strange to say, the noisy scampering of the rats in the wainscot began again.

By this time Malcolmson's mind was quite off the problem, and as a shrill cock-crow outside told him of the approach of morning, he went to bed and to sleep.

He slept so sound that he was not even waked by Mrs. Dempster coming in to make up his room. It was only when she had tidied up the place and got his breakfast ready and tapped on the screen which closed in his bed that he woke. He was a little tired still after his night's hard work, but a strong cup of tea soon freshened him up and, taking his book, he went out for his morning walk, bringing with him a few sandwiches lest he should not care to return till dinner-time. He found a quiet walk between high elms some way outside the town, and here he spent the greater part of the day studying his Laplace. On his return he looked in to see Mrs. Witham and to thank her for her kindness. When she saw him coming through the diamond-paned bay window of her sanctum she came out to meet him and asked him in. She looked at him searchingly and shook her head as she said:

"You must not overdo it, sir. You are paler this morning than you should be. Too late hours and too hard work on the brains isn't good for any man! But tell me, sir, how did you pass the night? Well, I hope? But, my heart! sir, I was glad when Mrs. Dempster told me this morning that you were all right and sleeping sound when she went in." "Oh, I was all right," he answered smiling, "The 'somethings' didn't worry me, as yet. Only the rats, and they had a circus, I tell you, all over the place. There was one wicked-looking old devil that sat up on my own chair by the fire, and wouldn't go till I took the poker to him, and then he ran up the rope of the alarm bell and got to somewhere up the wall or the ceiling—I couldn't see where, it was so dark."

"Mercy on us," said Mrs. Witham, "an old devil, and sitting on a chair by the fireside! Take care, sir! take care! There's many a true word spoken in jest."

"How do you mean? 'Pon my word, I don't understand."

"An old devil! The old devil, perhaps. There! sir, you needn't laugh," for Malcolmson had broken into a hearty peal. "You young folks think it easy to laugh at things that makes older ones shudder. Never mind, sir! never mind! Please God, you'll laugh all the time. It's what I wish you myself!" and the good lady beamed all over in sympathy with his enjoyment, her fears gone for a moment.

"Oh, forgive me," said Malcolmson presently. "Don't think me rude, but the idea was too much for me—that the old devil himself was on the chair last night!" And at the thought he laughed again. Then he went home to dinner.

This evening the scampering of the rats began earlier, indeed it had been going on before his arrival, and only ceased whilst his presence by its freshness disturbed them. After dinner he sat by the fire for a while and had a smoke, and then, having cleared his table, began to work as before. To-night the rats disturbed him more than they had done on the previous night.

How they scampered up and down and under and over! How they squeaked and scratched and gnawed! How they, getting bolder by degrees, came to the mouths of their holes and to the chinks and cracks and crannies in the wainscoting till their eyes shone like tiny lamps as the firelight rose and fell. But to him, now doubtless accustomed to them, their eyes were not wicked, only their playfulness touched him. Sometimes the boldest of them made sallies out on the floor or along the mouldings of the wainscot. Now and again as they disturbed him Malcolmson made a sound to frighten them, smiting the table with his hand or giving a fierce "Hsh, hsh," so that they fled straightway to their holes.

And so the early part of the night wore on, and despite the noise Malcolmson got more and more immersed in his work.

All at once he stopped, as on the previous night, being overcome by a sudden silence. There was not the faintest sound of gnaw, or scratch, or squeak. The silence was as of the grave.

He remembered the odd occurrence of the previous night, and instinctively he looked at the chair standing close by the fireside. And then a very odd sensation thrilled through him.

There, on the great old high-backed carved oak chair beside the fireplace sat the same enormous rat, steadily glaring at him with baleful eyes.

Instinctively he took the nearest thing to his hand, a book of logarithms, and flung it at it. The book was badly aimed and the rat did not stir, so again the poker performance of the previous night was repeated, and again the rat, being closely pursued, fled up the rope of the alarm bell. Strangely, too, the departure of this rat was instantly followed by the renewal of the noise made by the general rat community. On this occasion, as on the previous one, Malcolmson could not see at what part of the room the rat disappeared, for the green shade of his lamp left the upper part of the room in darkness and the fire had burned low.

On looking at his watch he found it was close on midnight, and, not sorry for the divertissement, he made up his fire and made himself his nightly pot of tea. He had got through a good spell of work, and thought himself entitled to a cigarette, and so he sat on the great carved oak chair before the fire and enjoyed it. Whilst smoking he began to think that he would like to know where the rat disappeared to, for he had certain ideas for the morrow not entirely disconnected with a rat-trap. Accordingly he lit another lamp and placed it so that it would shine well into the right-hand corner of the wall by the fireplace. Then he got all the books he had with him, and placed them handy to throw at the vermin. Finally he lifted the rope of the alarm bell and placed the end of it on the table, fixing the extreme end under the lamp. As he handled it he could not help noticing how pliable it was, especially for so strong a rope and one not in use. "You could hang a man with it," he thought to himself. When his preparations were made he looked around, and said complacently:

"There now, my friend, I think we shall learn something of you this time!" He began his work again, and though, as before, somewhat disturbed at first by the noise of the rats, soon lost himself in his proposition and problems.

Again he was called to his immediate surroundings suddenly. This time it might not have been the sudden silence only which took his attention; there was a slight movement of the rope, and the lamp moved. Without stirring, he looked to see if his pile of books was within range, and then cast his eye along the rope. As he looked he saw the great rat drop from the rope on the oak arm-chair and sit there glaring at him. He raised a book in his right hand, and taking careful aim, flung it at the rat. The latter, with a quick movement, sprang aside and dodged the missile. Then he took another book, and a third, and flung them one after the other at the rat, but each time unsuccessfully. At last, as he stood with a book poised in his hand to throw, the rat squeaked and seemed afraid. This made Malcolmson more than ever eager to strike, and the book flew and struck the rat a resounding blow. It gave a terrified squeak, and turning on his pursuer a look of terrible malevolence, ran up the chair-back and made a great jump to the rope of the alarm bell and ran up it like lightning. The lamp rocked under the sudden strain, but it was a heavy one and did not topple over. Malcolmson kept his eyes on the rat, and saw it by the light of the second lamp leap to a moulding of the wainscot and disappear through a hole in one of the great pictures which hung on the wall, obscured and invisible through its coating of dirt and dust.

"I shall look up my friend's habitation in the morning," said the student, as he went over to collect his books. "The third picture from the fireplace, I shall not forget." He picked up the books one by one, commenting on them as he lifted them. Conic Sections he does not mind, nor Cycloid Oscillations, nor the Principia, nor Quaternions, nor Thermodynamics. Now for a look at the book that fetched him!" Malcolmson took it up and looked at it. As he did so he started, and a sudden pallor overspread his face. He looked round uneasily and shivered slightly, as he murmured to himself:

"The Bible my mother gave me! What an odd coincidence." He sat down to work again, and the rats in the wainscot renewed their gambols. They did not disturb him, however; somehow their presence gave him a sense of companionship. But he could not attend to his work, and after striving to master the subject on which he was engaged gave it up in despair, and went to bed as the first streak of dawn stole in through the eastern window.

He slept heavily but uneasily, and dreamed much, and when Mrs. Dempster woke him late in the morning he seemed ill at ease, and for a few minutes did not seem to realize exactly where he was. His first request rather surprised the servant.

"Mrs. Dempster, when I am out to-day I wish you would get the steps and dust or wash those pictures—specially that one the third from the fireplace—I want to see what they are."

Late in the afternoon Malcolmson worked at his books in the shaded walk, and the cheerfulness of the previous day came back to him as the day wore on, and he found that his reading was progressing well. He had worked out to a satisfactory conclusion all the problems which had as yet baffled him, and it was in a state of jubilation that he paid a visit to Mrs. Witham at "The Good Traveller." He found a stranger in the cosy sitting-room with the landlady, who was introduced to him as Dr. Thornhill. She was not quite at ease, and this, combined with the doctor's plunging at once into a series of questions, made Malcolmson come to the conclusion that his presence was not an accident, so without preliminary he said:

"Dr. Thornhill, I shall with pleasure answer you any question you may choose to ask me if you will answer me one question first."

The doctor seemed surprised, but he smiled and answered at once, "Done! What is it?"

"Did Mrs. Witham ask you to come here and see me and advise me?"

Dr. Thornhill for a moment was taken aback, and Mrs. Witham got fiery red and turned away, but the doctor was a frank and ready man, and he answered at once and openly:

"She did, but she didn't intend you to know it. I suppose it was my clumsy haste that made you suspect. She told me that she did not like the idea of your being in that house all by yourself, and that she thought you took too much strong tea. In fact, she wants me to advise you, if possible, to give up the tea and the very late hours. I was a keen student in my time, so I suppose I may take the liberty of a college man, and without offence, advise you not quite as a stranger."

Malcolmson with a bright smile held out his hand. "Shake—as they say in America," he said. "I must thank you for your kindness, and Mrs. Witham too, and your kindness deserves a return on my part. I promise to take no more strong tea—no tea at all till you let me—and I shall go to bed to-night at one o'clock at latest. Will that do?"

"Capital," said the doctor. "Now tell us all that you noticed in the old house," and so Malcolmson then and there told in minute detail all that had happened in the last two nights. He was interrupted every now and then by some exclamation from Mrs. Witham, till finally when he told of the episode of the Bible the landlady's pent-up emotions found vent in a shriek, and it was not till a stiff glass of brandy and water had been administered that she grew composed again. Dr. Thornhill listened with a face of growing gravity, and when the narrative was complete and Mrs. Witham had been restored he asked:

"The rat always went up the rope of the alarm bell?"

"Always."

"I suppose you know," said the Doctor after a pause, "what that rope is?"

"No?"

"It is," said the Doctor slowly, "the very rope which the hangman used for all the victims of the Judge's judicial rancour!" Here he was interrupted by another scream from Mrs. Witham, and steps had to be taken for her recovery. Malcolmson having looked at his watch, and found that it was close to his dinner-hour, had gone home before her complete recovery.

When Mrs. Witham was herself again she almost assailed the Doctor with angry questions as to what he meant by putting such horrible ideas into the poor young man's mind. "He has quite enough there already to upset him," she added.

Dr. Thornhill replied:

"My dear madam, I had a distinct purpose in it! I wanted to draw his attention to the bell-rope, and to fix it there. It may be that he is in a highly over-wrought state, and has been studying too much, although I am bound to say that he seems as sound and healthy a young man, mentally and bodily, as ever I saw—but then the rats—and that suggestion of the devil." The doctor shook his head and went on. "I would have offered to go and stay the first night with him but that I felt sure it would have been a cause of offence. He may get in the night some strange fright or hallucination, and if he does I want him to pull that rope. All alone as he is it will give us warning, and we may reach him in time to be of service. I shall be sitting up pretty late to-night and shall keep my ears open. Do not be alarmed if Benchurch gets a surprise before morning."

"Oh, Doctor, what do you mean? What do you mean?"

"I mean this, that possibly—nay, more probably—we shall hear the great alarm-bell from the Judge's House to-night," and the Doctor made about an effective an exit as could be thought of.

When Malcolmson arrived home he found that it was a little after his usual time, and Mrs. Dempster had gone away—the rules of Greenhow's Charity were not to be neglected. He was glad to see that the place was bright and tidy with a cheerful fire and a well-trimmed lamp. The evening was colder than might have been expected in April, and a heavy wind was blowing with such rapidly-increasing strength that there was every promise of a storm during the night. For a few minutes after his entrance the noise of the rats ceased, but so soon as they became accustomed to his presence they began again. He was glad to hear them, for he felt once more the feeling of companionship in their noise, and his mind ran back to the strange fact that they only ceased to manifest themselves when the other—the great rat with the baleful eyes—came upon the scene. The reading- lamp only was lit and its green shade kept the ceiling and the upper part of the room in darkness so that the cheerful light from the hearth spreading over the floor and shining on the white cloth laid over the end of the table was warm and cheery. Malcolmson sat down to his dinner with a good appetite and a buoyant spirit. After his dinner and a cigarette he sat steadily down to work, determined not to let anything disturb him, for he remembered his promise to the doctor, and made up his mind to make the best of the time at his disposal.

For an hour or so he worked all right, and then his thoughts began to wander from his books. The actual circumstances around him, and the calls on his physical attention, and his nervous susceptibility were not to be denied. By this time the wind had become a gale, and the gale a storm. The old house, solid though it was, seemed to shake to its foundation, and the storm roared and raged through its many chimneys and its queer old gables, producing strange, unearthly sounds in the empty rooms and corridors. Even the great alarm-bell on the roof must have felt the force of the wind, for the rope rose and fell slightly, as though the bell were moved a little from time to time, and the limber rope fell on the oak floor with a hard and hollow sound.

As Malcolmson listened to it he bethought himself of the doctor's words, "It is the rope which the hangman used for the victims of the Judge's judicial rancour," and he went over to the corner of the fireplace and took it in his hand to look at it. There seemed a sort of deadly interest in it, and as he stood there he lost himself for a moment in speculation as to who these victims were, and the grim wish of the Judge to have such a ghastly relic ever under his eyes. As he stood there the swaying of the bell on the roof still lifted the rope now and again, but presently there came a new sensation—a sort of tremor in the rope, as though something was moving along it.

Looking up instinctively Malcolmson saw the great rat coming slowly down towards him, glaring at him steadily. He dropped the rope and started back with a muttered curse, and the rat turning ran up the slope again and disappeared, and at the same instant Malcolmson became conscious that the noise of the other rats, which had ceased for a while, began again.

All this set him thinking, and it occurred to him that he had not investigated the lair of the rat or looked at the pictures, as he had intended. He lit the other lamp without the shade, and, holding it up went and stood opposite the third picture from the fireplace on the right-hand side where he had seen the rat disappear on the previous night.

At the first glance he started back so suddenly that he almost dropped the lamp, and a deadly pallor overspread his face.

His knees shook, and heavy drops of sweat came on his forehead, and he trembled like an aspen. But he was young and plucky, and pulled himself together, and after the pause of a few seconds stepped forward again, raised the lamp, and examined the picture which had been dusted and washed, and now stood out clearly.

It was of a judge dressed in his robes of scarlet and ermine. His face was strong and merciless, evil, crafty and vindictive, with a sensual mouth, hooked nose of ruddy colour, and shaped like the beak of a bird of prey. The rest of the face was of a cadaverous colour. The eyes were of peculiar brilliance and with a terribly malignant expression. As he looked at them, Malcolmson grew cold, for he saw there the very counterpart of the eyes of the great rat. The lamp almost fell from his hand, he saw the rat with its baleful eyes peering out through the hole in the corner of the picture, and noted the sudden cessation of the noise of the other rats. However, he pulled himself together, and went on with his examination of the picture.

The Judge was seated in a great high-backed carved oak chair, on the right-hand side of a great stone fireplace where, in the corner, a rope hung down from the ceiling, its end lying coiled on the floor. With a feeling of something like horror, Malcolmson recognized the scene of the room as it stood, and gazed around him in an awestruck manner as though he expected to find some strange presence behind him. Then he looked over to the corner of the fireplace—and with a loud cry he let the lamp fall from his hand.

There, in the judge's arm-chair, with the rope hanging behind, sat the rat with the Judge's baleful eyes, now intensified as with a fiendish leer. Save for the howling of the storm without there was silence.

The fallen lamp recalled Malcolmson to himself. Fortunately it was of metal, and so the oil was not spilt. However, the practical need of attending to it settled at once his nervous apprehensions. When he had turned it out, he wiped his brow and thought for a moment.

"This will not do," he said to himself. "If I go on like this I shall become a crazy fool. This must stop! I promised the doctor I would not take tea. Faith, he was pretty right! My nerves must have been getting into a queer state. Funny I did not notice it. I never felt better in my life. However, it is all right now, and I shall not be such a fool again."

Then he mixed himself a good stiff glass of brandy and water and resolutely sat down to his work.

It was nearly an hour when he looked up from his book, disturbed by the sudden stillness. Without, the wind howled and roared louder then ever, and the rain drove in sheets against the windows, beating like hail on the glass, but within there was no sound whatever save the echo of the wind as it roared in the great chimney, and now and then a hiss as a few raindrops found their way down the chimney in a lull of the storm. The fire had fallen low and had ceased to flame, though it threw out a red glow. Malcolmson listened attentively, and presently heard a thin, squeaking noise, very faint. It came from the corner of the room where the rope hung down, and he thought it was the creaking of the rope on the floor as the swaying of the bell raised and lowered it. Looking up, however, he saw in the dim light the great rat clinging to the rope and gnawing it. The rope was already nearly gnawed through—he could see the lighter colour where the strands were laid bare. As he looked the job was completed, and the severed end of the rope fell clattering on the oaken floor, whilst for an instant the great rat remained like a knob or tassel at the end of the rope, which now began to sway to and fro. Malcolmson felt for a moment another pang of terror as he thought that now the possibility of calling the outer world to his assistance was cut off, but an intense anger took its place, and seizing the book he was reading he hurled it at the rat. The blow was well-aimed, but before the missile could reach him the rat dropped off and struck the floor with a soft thud. Malcolmson instantly rushed over towards him, but it darted away and disappeared in the darkness of the shadows of the room. Malcolmson felt that his work was over for the night, and determined then and there to vary the monotony of the proceedings by a hunt for the rat, and took off the green shade of the lamp so as to insure a wider spreading light. As he did so the gloom of the upper part of the room was relieved, and in the new flood of light, great by comparison with the previous darkness, the pictures on the wall stood out boldly.

From where he stood, Malcolmson saw right opposite to him the third picture on the wall from the right of the fireplace. He rubbed his eyes in surprise, and then a great fear began to come upon him.

In the centre of the picture was a great irregular patch of brown canvas, as fresh as when it was stretched on the frame. The background was as before, with chair and chimney-corner and rope, but the figure of the Judge had disappeared.

Malcolmson, almost in a chill of horror, turned slowly round, and then he began to shake and tremble like a man in a palsy. His strength seemed to have left him, and he was incapable of action or movement, hardly even of thought. He could only see and hear.

There, on the great high-backed carved oak chair sat the judge in his robes of scarlet and ermine, with his baleful eyes glaring vindictively, and a smile of triumph on the resolute cruel mouth, as he lifted with his hands a black cap. Malcolmson felt as if the blood was running from his heart, as one does in moments of prolonged suspense. There was a singing in his ears. Without, he could hear the roar and howl of the tempest, and through it, swept on the storm, came the striking of midnight by the great chimes in the market-place. He stood for a space of time that seemed to him endless still as a statue, and with wide-open, horror-struck eyes, breathless. As the clock struck, so the smile of triumph on the Judge's face intensified, and at the last stroke of midnight he placed the black cap on his head.

Slowly and deliberately the Judge rose from his chair and picked up the piece of rope of the alarm bell which lay on the floor, drew it through his hands as if he enjoyed its touch and then deliberately began to knot one end of it, fashioning it into a noose. This he tightened and tested with his foot, pulling hard at it till he was satisfied and then making a running noose of it, which he held in his hand. Then he began to move along the table on the opposite side of Malcolmson keeping his eyes on him until he had passed him, when with a quick movement he stood in front of the door. Malcolmson then began to feel that he was trapped, and tried to think of what he should do. There was some fascination in the Judge's eyes, which he never took off him, and he had, perforce, to look. He saw the Judge approach—still keeping between him and the door—and raise the noose and throw it towards him as if to entangle him. With a great effort he made a quick movement to one side, and saw the rope fall beside him, and heard it strike the oaken floor. Again the Judge raised the noose and tried to ensnare him, ever keeping his baleful eyes fixed on him, and each time by a mighty effort the student just managed to evade it. So this went on for many times, the Judge seeming never discouraged nor discomposed at failure, but playing as a cat does with a mouse. At last in despair, which had reached its climax, Malcolmson cast a quick glance round him. The lamp seemed to have blazed up, and there was a fairly good light in the room. At the many rat-holes and in the chinks and crannies of the wainscot he saw the rats' eyes, and this aspect, that was purely physical, gave him a gleam of comfort. He looked round and saw that the rope of the great alarm bell was laden with rats. Every inch of it was covered with them, and more and more were pouring through the small circular hole in the ceiling whence it emerged, so that with their weight the bell was beginning to sway.

Hark! it had swayed till the clapper had touched the bell. The sound was but a tiny one, but the bell was only beginning to sway, and it would increase.

At the sound the Judge, who had been keeping his eyes fixed on Malcolmson, looked up, and a scowl of diabolical anger overspread his face. His eyes fairly glowed like hot coals, and he stamped his foot with a sound that seemed to make the house shake. A dreadful peal of thunder broke overhead as he raised the rope again, whilst the rats kept running up and down the rope as though working against time. This time, instead of throwing it, he drew close to his victim, and held open the noose as he approached. As he came closer there seemed something paralyzing in his very presence, and Malcolmson stood rigid as a corpse. He felt the Judge's icy fingers touch his throat as he adjusted the rope. The noose tightened—tightened. Then the Judge, taking the rigid form of the student in his arms, carried him over and placed him standing in the oak chair, and stepping up beside him, put his hand up and caught the end of the swaying rope of the alarm-bell. As he raised his hand the rats fled squeaking and disappeared through the hole in the ceiling. Taking the end of the noose which was round Malcolmson's neck he tied it to the hanging bell-rope, and then descending pulled away the chair.

When the alarm-bell of the Judge's House began to sound a crowd soon assembled. Lights and torches of various kinds appeared, and soon a silent crowd was hurrying to the spot. They knocked loudly at the door, but there was no reply. Then they burst in the door, and poured into the great dining-room, the doctor at the head.

There at the end of the rope of the great alarm-bell hung the body of the student, and on the face of the Judge in the picture was a malignant smile.

The Juryman by John Galsworthy

"Don't you see, brother, I was reading yesterday the Gospel about Christ, the little Father; how He suffered, how He walked on the earth. I suppose you have heard about it?"

"Indeed, I have," replied Stepanuitch; "but we are people in darkness; we can't read."—Tolstoy.

I.

Mr. Henry Bosengate, of the London Stock Exchange, seated himself in his car that morning during the great war with a sense of injury. Major in a Volunteer Corps; member of all the local committees; lending this very car to the neighbouring hospital, at times even driving it himself for their benefit; subscribing to funds, so far as his diminished income permitted, he was conscious of being an asset to the country, and one whose time could not be wasted with impunity. To be summoned to sit on a jury at the local assizes, and not even the grand jury at that! It was in the nature of an outrage.

Strong and upright, with hazel eyes and dark eyebrows, pinkish-brown cheeks, a forehead white, well-shaped, and getting high, with greyish hair glossy and well-brushed, and a trim moustache, he might have been taken for that colonel of Volunteers which indeed he was in a fair way of becoming.

His wife had followed him out under the porch, and stood bracing her supple body clothed in lilac linen. Red rambler roses formed a sort of crown to her dark head; her ivory-coloured face had in it just a suggestion of the Japanese.

Mr. Bosengate spoke through the whirr of the engine:

"I don't expect to be late, dear. This business is ridiculous. There oughtn't to be any crime in these days."

His wife, her name was Kathleen, smiled. She looked very pretty and cool, Mr. Bosengate thought. To him bound on this dull and stuffy business everything he owned seemed pleasant, the geranium beds beside the gravel drive, his long, red-brick house mellowing decorously in its creepers and ivy, the little clock-tower over stables now converted to a garage, the dovecote, masking at the other end the conservatory which adjoined the billiard-room. Close to the red-brick lodge his two children, Kate and Harry, ran out from under the acacia trees, and waved to him, scrambling bare-legged on to the low, red, ivy-covered wall which guarded his domain of eleven acres. Mr. Bosengate waved back, thinking: 'Jolly couple, by Jove, they are!' Above their heads, through the trees, he could see right away to some Downs, faint in the July heat haze. And he thought: 'Pretty a spot as one could have got, so close to Town!'

Despite the war he had enjoyed these last two years more than any of the ten since he built "Charmleigh" and settled down to semi-rural domesticity with his young wife. There had been a certain piquancy, a savour added to existence, by the country's peril, and all the public service and sacrifice it demanded. His chauffeur was gone, and one gardener did the work of three. He enjoyed-positively enjoyed, his committee work; even the serious decline of business and increase of taxation had not much worried one continually conscious of the national crisis and his own part therein. The country had wanted waking up, wanted a lesson in effort and economy; and the feeling that he had not spared himself in these strenuous times, had given a zest to those quiet pleasures of bed and board which, at his age, even the most patriotic could retain with a good conscience. He had denied himself many things, new clothes, presents for Kathleen and the children, travel, and that pine-apple house which he had been on the point of building when the war broke out; new wine, too, and cigars, and membership of the two Clubs which he had never used in the old days. The hours had seemed fuller and longer, sleep better earned, wonderful, the things one could do without when put to it! He turned the car into the high road, driving dreamily for he was in plenty of time. The war was going pretty well now; he was no fool optimist, but now that conscription was in force, one might reasonably hope for its end within a year. Then there would be a boom, and one might let oneself go a little. Visions of theatres and supper with his wife at the Savoy afterwards, and cosy night drives back into the sweet-smelling country behind your own chauffeur once more teased a fancy which even now did not soar beyond the confines of domestic pleasures. He pictured his wife in new dresses by Jay, she was fifteen years younger than himself, and "paid for dressing" as they said. He had always delighted as men older than their wives will in the admiration she excited from others not privileged to enjoy her charms. Her rather queer and ironical beauty, her cool irreproachable wifeliness, was a constant balm to him. They would give dinner parties again, have their friends down from town, and he would once more enjoy sitting at the foot of the dinner table while Kathleen sat at the head, with the light soft on her ivory shoulders, behind flowers she had arranged in that original way of hers, and fruit which he had grown in his hot-houses; once more he would take legitimate interest in the wine he offered to his guests, once more stock that Chinese cabinet wherein he kept cigars. Yes, there was a certain satisfaction in these days of privation, if only from the anticipation they created.

The sprinkling of villas had become continuous on either side of the high road; and women going out to shop, tradesmen's boys delivering victuals, young men in khaki, began to abound. Now and then a limping or bandaged form would pass, some bit of human wreckage; and Mr. Bosengate would think mechanically: 'Another of those poor devils! Wonder if we've had his case before us!'

Running his car into the best hotel garage of the little town, he made his way leisurely over to the court. It stood back from the market-place, and was already lapped by a sea of persons having, as in the outer ring at race meetings, an air of business at which one must not be caught out, together with a soaked or flushed appearance. Mr. Bosengate could not resist putting his handkerchief to his nose. He had carefully drenched it with lavender water, and to this fact owed, perhaps, his immunity from the post of foreman on the jury, for, say what you will about the English, they have a deep instinct for affairs.

He found himself second in the front row of the jury box, and through the odour of "Sanitas" gazed at the judge's face expressionless up there, for all the world like a bewigged bust. His fellows in the box had that appearance of falling between two classes characteristic of jurymen. Mr. Bosengate was not impressed. On one side of him the foreman sat, a prominent upholsterer, known in the town as "Gentleman Fox." His dark and beautifully brushed and oiled hair and moustache, his radiant linen, gold watch and chain, the white piping to his waistcoat, and a habit of never saying "Sir" had long marked him out from commoner men; he undertook to bury people too, to save them trouble; and was altogether superior. On the other side Mr. Bosengate had one of those men, who, except when they sit on juries, are never seen without a little brown bag, and the appearance of having been interrupted in a drink. Pale and shiny, with large loose eyes shifting from side to side, he had an underdone voice and uneasy flabby hands. Mr. Bosengate disliked sitting next to him. Beyond this commercial traveller sat a dark pale young man with spectacles; beyond him again, a short old man with grey moustache, mutton chops, and innumerable wrinkles; and the front row was completed by a chemist. The three immediately behind, Mr. Bosengate did not thoroughly master; but the three at the end of the second row he learned in their order of an oldish man in a grey suit, given to winking; an inanimate person with the mouth of a moustachioed codfish, over whose long bald crown three wisps of damp hair were carefully arranged; and a dried, dapperish, clean-shorn man, whose mouth seemed terrified lest it should be surprised without a smile. Their first and second verdicts were recorded without the necessity for withdrawal, and Mr. Bosengate was already sleepy when the third case was called. The sight of khaki revived his drooping attention. But what a weedy-looking specimen! This prisoner had a truly nerveless pitiable dejected air. If he had ever had a military bearing it had shrunk into him during his confinement. His ill-shaped brown tunic, whose little brass buttons seemed trying to keep smiling, struck Mr. Bosengate as ridiculously short, used though he was to such things. 'Absurd,' he thought 'Lumbago! Just where they ought to be covered!' Then the officer and gentleman stirred in him, and he added to himself: 'Still, there must be some distinction made!' The little soldier's visage had once perhaps been tanned, but was now the colour of dark dough; his large brown eyes with white showing below the iris, as so often in the eyes of very nervous people, wandered from face to face, of judge, counsel, jury, and public. There were hollows in his cheeks, his dark hair looked damp; around his neck he wore a bandage. The commercial traveller on Mr. Bosengate's left turned, and whispered: "Felo de se! My hat! what a guy!" Mr. Bosengate pretended not to hear, he could not bear that fellow! and slowly wrote on a bit of paper: "Owen Lewis." Welsh! Well, he looked it, not at all an English face. Attempted suicide, not at all an English crime! Suicide implied surrender, a putting-up of hands to Fate, to say nothing of the religious aspect of the matter. And suicide in khaki seemed to Mr. Bosengate particularly abhorrent; like turning tail in face of the enemy; almost meriting the fate of a deserter. He looked at the prisoner, trying not to give way to this prejudice. And the prisoner seemed to look at him, though this, perhaps, was fancy.

The Counsel for the prosecution, a little, alert, grey, decided man, above military age, began detailing the circumstances of the crime. Mr. Bosengate, though not particularly sensitive to atmosphere, could perceive a sort of current running through the Court. It was as if jury and public were thinking rhythmically in obedience to the same unexpressed prejudice of which he himself was conscious. Even the Caesar-like pale face up there, presiding, seemed in its ironic serenity responding to that current.

"Gentlemen of the jury, before I call my evidence, I direct your attention to the bandage the accused is still wearing. He gave himself this wound with his Army razor, adding, if I may say so, insult to the injury he was inflicting on his country. He pleads not guilty; and before the magistrates he said that absence from his wife was preying on his mind" the advocate's close lips widened "Well, gentlemen, if such an excuse is to weigh with us in these days, I'm sure I don't know what's to happen to the Empire."

'No, by George!' thought Mr. Bosengate.

The evidence of the first witness, a room-mate who had caught the prisoner's hand, and of the sergeant, who had at once been summoned, was conclusive and he began to cherish a hope that they would get through without withdrawing, and he would be home before five. But then a hitch occurred. The regimental doctor failed to respond when his name was called; and the judge having for the first time that day showed himself capable of human emotion, intimated that he would adjourn until the morrow.

Mr. Bosengate received the announcement with equanimity. He would be home even earlier! And gathering up the sheets of paper he had scribbled on, he put them in his pocket and got up. The would-be suicide was being taken out of the court, a shambling drab figure with shoulders hunched. What good were men like that in these days! What good! The prisoner looked up. Mr. Bosengate encountered in full the gaze of those large brown eyes, with the white showing underneath. What a suffering, wretched, pitiful face! A man had no business to give you a look like that! The prisoner passed on down the stairs, and vanished. Mr. Bosengate went out and across the market place to the garage of the hotel where he had left his car. The sun shone fiercely and he thought: 'I must do some watering in the garden.' He brought the car out, and was about to start the engine, when someone passing said: "Good evenin'. Seedy-lookin' beggar that last prisoner, ain't he? We don't want men of that stamp." It was his neighbour on the jury, the commercial traveller, in a straw hat, with a little brown bag already in his hand and the froth of an interrupted drink on his moustache. Answering curtly: "Good evening!" and thinking: 'Nor of yours, my friend!' Mr. Bosengate started the car with unnecessary clamour. But as if brought back to life by the commercial traveller's remark, the prisoner's figure seemed to speed along too, turning up at Mr. Bosengate his pitifully unhappy eyes. Want of his wife! queer excuse that for trying to put it out of his power ever to see her again! Why! Half a loaf, even a slice, was better than no bread. Not many of that neurotic type in the Army, thank Heaven! The lugubrious figure vanished, and Mr. Bosengate pictured instead the form of his own wife bending over her "Gloire de Dijon roses" in the rosery, where she generally worked a little before tea now that they were short of gardeners. He saw her, as often he had seen her, raise herself and stand, head to one side, a gloved hand on her slender hip, gazing as it were ironically from under drooped lids at buds which did not come out fast enough. And the word 'Caline,' for he was something of a French scholar, shot through his mind: 'Kathleen, Caline!' If he found her there when he got in, he would steal up on the grass and ah! but with great care not to crease her dress or disturb her hair! 'If only she weren't quite so self-contained,' he thought; 'It's like a cat you can't get near, not really near!'

The car, returning faster than it had come down that morning, had already passed the outskirt villas, and was breasting the hill to where, among fields and the old trees, Charmleigh lay apart from commoner life. Turning into his drive, Mr. Bosengate thought with a certain surprise: 'I wonder what she does think of! I wonder!' He put his gloves and hat down in the outer hall and went into the lavatory, to dip his face in cool water and wash it with sweet-smelling soap, delicious revenge on the unclean atmosphere in which he had been stewing so many hours. He came out again into the hall dazed by soap and the mellowed light, and a voice from half-way up the stairs said: "Daddy! Look!" His little daughter was standing up there with one hand on the banisters. She scrambled on to them and came sliding down, her frock up to her eyes, and her holland knickers to her middle. Mr. Bosengate said mildly:

"Well, that's elegant!"

"Tea's in the summer-house. Mummy's waiting. Come on!"

With her hand in his, Mr. Bosengate went on, through the drawing-room, long and cool, with sun-blinds down, through the billiard-room, high and cool, through the conservatory, green and sweet-smelling, out on to the terrace and the upper lawn. He had never felt such sheer exhilarated joy in his home surroundings, so cool, glistening and green under the July sun; and he said:

"Well, Kit, what have you all been doing?"

"I've fed my rabbits and Harry's; and we've been in the attic; Harry got his leg through the skylight."

Mr. Bosengate drew in his breath with a hiss.

"It's all right, Daddy; we got it out again, it's only grazed the skin. And we've been making swabs, I made seventeen, Mummy made thirty-three, and then she went to the hospital. Did you put many men in prison?"

Mr. Bosengate cleared his throat. The question seemed to him untimely.

"Only two."

"What's it like in prison, Daddy?"

Mr. Bosengate, who had no more knowledge than his little daughter, replied in an absent voice:

"Not very nice."

They were passing under a young oak tree, where the path wound round to the rosery and summer-house. Something shot down and clawed Mr. Bosengate's neck. His little daughter began to hop and suffocate with laughter.

"Oh, Daddy! Aren't you caught! I led you on purpose!"

Looking up, Mr. Bosengate saw his small son lying along a low branch above him, like the leopard he was declaring himself to be (for fear of error), and thought blithely: 'What an active little chap it is!' "Let me drop on your shoulders, Daddy, like they do on the deer."

"Oh, yes! Do be a deer, Daddy!"

Mr. Bosengate did not see being a deer; his hair had just been brushed. But he entered the rosery buoyantly between his offspring. His wife was standing precisely as he had imagined her, in a pale blue frock open at the neck, with a narrow black band round the waist, and little accordion pleats below. She looked her coolest. Her smile, when she turned her head, hardly seemed to take Mr. Bosengate seriously enough. He placed his lips below one of her half-drooped eyelids. She even smelled of roses. His children began to dance round their mother, and Mr. Bosengate, firmly held between them, was also compelled to do this, until she said:

"When you've quite done, let's have tea!"

It was not the greeting he had imagined coming along in the car. Earwigs were plentiful in the summer-house, used perhaps twice a year, but indispensable to every country residence and Mr. Bosengate was not sorry for the excuse to get out again. Though all was so pleasant, he felt oddly restless, rather suffocated; and lighting his pipe, began to move about among the roses, blowing tobacco at the greenfly; in war-time one was never quite idle! And suddenly he said:

"We're trying a wretched Tommy at the assizes."

His wife looked up from a rose.

"What for?"

"Attempted suicide."

"Why did he?"

"Can't stand the separation from his wife."

She looked at him, gave a low laugh, and said:

"Oh dear!"

Mr. Bosengate was puzzled. Why did she laugh? He looked round, saw that the children were gone, took his pipe from his mouth, and approached her.

"You look very pretty," he said. "Give me a kiss!"

His wife bent her body forward from the waist, and pushed her lips out till they touched his moustache. Mr. Bosengate felt a sensation as if he had arisen from breakfast, without having eaten marmalade. He mastered it, and said:

"That jury are a rum lot."

His wife's eyelids flickered. "I wish women sat on juries."

"Why?"

"It would be an experience."

Not the first time she had used that curious expression! Yet her life was far from dull, so far as he could see; with the new interests created by the war, and the constant calls on her time made by the perfection of their home life, she had a useful and busy existence. Again the random thought passed through him: 'But she never tells me anything!' And suddenly that lugubrious khaki-clad figure started up among the rose bushes. "We've got a lot to be thankful for!" he said abruptly. "I must go to work!" His wife, raising one eyebrow, smiled. "And I to weep!" Mr. Bosengate laughed, she had a pretty wit! And stroking his comely moustache where it had been kissed, he moved out into the sunshine. All the evening, throughout his labours, not inconsiderable, for this jury business had put him behind time, he was afflicted by that restless pleasure in his surroundings; would break off in mowing the lower lawn to look at the house through the trees; would leave his study and committee papers, to cross into the drawing-room and sniff its dainty fragrance; paid a special good-night visit to the children having supper in the schoolroom; pottered in and out from his dressing room to admire his wife while she was changing for dinner; dined with his mind perpetually on the next course; talked volubly of the war; and in the billiard room afterwards, smoking the pipe which had taken the place of his cigar, could not keep still, but roamed about, now in conservatory, now in the drawing-room, where his wife and the governess were still making swabs. It seemed to him that he could not have enough of anything. About eleven o'clock he strolled out beautiful night, only just dark enough, under the new arrangement with Time and went down to the little round fountain below the terrace. His wife was playing the piano. Mr. Bosengate looked at the water and the flat dark water lily leaves which floated there; looked up at the house, where only narrow chinks of light showed, because of the Lighting Order. The dreamy music drifted out; there was a scent of heliotrope. He moved a few steps back, and sat in the children's swing under an old lime tree. Jolly blissful in the warm, bloomy dark! Of all hours of the day, this before going to bed was perhaps the pleasantest. He saw the light go up in his wife's bed room, unscreened for a full minute, and thought: 'Aha! If I did my duty as a special, I should "strafe" her for that.' She came to the window, her figure lighted, hands up to the back of her head, so that her bare arms gleamed. Mr. Bosengate wafted her a kiss, knowing he could not be seen. 'Lucky chap!' he mused; 'she's a great joy!' Up went her arm, down came the blind the house was dark again. He drew a long breath. 'Another ten minutes,' he thought, 'then I'll go in and shut up. By Jove! The limes are beginning to smell already!' And, the better to take in that acme of his well-being, he tilted the swing, lifted his feet from the ground, and swung himself toward the scented blossoms. He wanted to whelm his senses in their perfume, and closed his eyes. But instead of the domestic vision he expected, the face of the little Welsh soldier, hare-eyed, shadowy, pinched and dark and pitiful, started up with such disturbing vividness that he opened his eyes again at once. Curse! The fellow almost haunted one! Where would he be now poor little devil! lying in his cell, thinking—thinking of his wife! Feeling suddenly morbid, Mr. Bosengate arrested the swing and stood up. Absurd! all his well-being and mood of warm anticipation had deserted him! 'A damned world!' he thought. 'Such a lot of misery! Why should I have to sit in judgment on that poor beggar, and condemn him?' He moved up on to the terrace and walked briskly, to rid himself of this disturbance before going in. 'That commercial traveller chap,' he thought, 'the rest of those fellows, they see nothing!' And, abruptly turning up the three stone steps, he entered the conservatory, locked it, passed into the billiard room, and drank his barley water. One of the pictures was hanging crooked; he went up to put it straight. Still life. Grapes and apples, and lobsters! They struck him as odd for the first time. Why lobsters? The whole picture seemed dead and oily. He turned off the light, and went upstairs, passed his wife's door, into his own room, and undressed. Clothed in his pyjamas he opened the door between the rooms. By the light coming from his own he could see her dark head on the pillow. Was she asleep? No, not asleep, certainly. The moment of fruition had come; the crowning of his pride and pleasure in his home. But he continued to stand there. He had suddenly no pride, no pleasure, no desire; nothing but a sort of dull resentment against everything. He turned back; shut the door, and slipping between the heavy curtains and his open window, stood looking out at the night. 'Full of misery!' he thought. 'Full of damned misery!'

II.

Filing into the jury box next morning, Mr. Bosengate collided slightly with a short juryman, whose square figure and square head of stiff yellow-red hair he had only vaguely noticed the day before. The man looked angry, and Mr. Bosengate thought: 'An ill-bred dog, that!'

He sat down quickly, and, to avoid further recognition of his fellows, gazed in front of him. His appearance on Saturdays was always military, by reason of the route march of his Volunteer Corps in the afternoon. Gentleman Fox, who belonged to the corps too, was also looking square; but that commercial traveller on his other side seemed more louche, and as if surprised in immorality, than ever; only the proximity of Gentleman Fox on the other side kept Mr. Bosengate from shrinking. Then he saw the prisoner being brought in, shadowy and dark behind the brightness of his buttons, and he experienced a sort of shock, this figure was so exactly that which had several times started up in his mind. Somehow he had expected a fresh sight of the fellow to dispel and disprove what had been haunting him, had expected to find him just an outside phenomenon, not, as it were, a part of his own life. And he gazed at the carven immobility of the judge's face, trying to steady himself, as a drunken man will, by looking at a light. The regimental doctor, unabashed by the judge's comment on his absence the day before, gave his evidence like a man who had better things to do, and the case for the prosecution was forthwith rounded in by a little speech from counsel. The matter, he said, was clear as daylight. Those who wore His Majesty's uniform, charged with the responsibility and privilege of defending their country, were no more entitled to desert their regiments by taking their own lives than they were entitled to desert in any other way. He asked for a conviction. Mr. Bosengate felt a sympathetic shuffle passing through all feet; the judge was speaking:

"Prisoner, you can either go into the witness box and make your statement on oath, in which case you may be cross-examined on it; or you can make your statement there from the dock, in which case you will not be cross-examined. Which do you elect to do?"

"From here, my lord."

Seeing him now full face, and, as it might be, come to life in the effort to convey his feelings, Mr. Bosengate had suddenly a quite different impression of the fellow. It was as if his khaki had fallen off, and he had stepped out of his own shadow, a live and quivering creature. His pinched clean-shaven face seemed to have an irregular, wilder, hairier look, his large nervous brown eyes darkened and glowed; he jerked his shoulders, his arms, his whole body, like a man suddenly freed from cramp or a suit of armour.

He spoke, too, in a quick, crisp, rather high voice, pinching his consonants a little, sharpening his vowels, like a true Welshman.

"My lord and misters the jury," he said: "I was a hairdresser when the call came on me to join the army. I had a little home and a wife. I never thought what it would be like to be away from them, I surely never did; and I'm ashamed to be speaking it out like this, how it can squeeze and squeeze a man, how it can prey on your mind, when you're nervous like I am. 'Tis not everyone that cares for his home, there's lots o' them never wants to see their wives again. But for me 'tis like being shut up in a cage, it is!" Mr. Bosengate saw daylight between the skinny fingers of the man's hand thrown out with a jerk. "I cannot bear it shut up away from wife and home like what you are in the army. So when I took my razor that morning I was wild an' I wouldn't be here now but for that man catching my hand. There was no reason in it, I'm willing to confess. It was foolish; but wait till you get feeling like what I was, and see how it draws you. Misters the jury, don't send me back to prison; it is worse still there. If you have wives you will know what it is like for lots of us; only some is more nervous than others. I swear to you, sirs, I could not help it -?" Again the little man flung out his hand, his whole thin body shook and Mr. Bosengate felt the same sensation as when he drove his car over a dog "Misters the jury, I hope you may never in your lives feel as I've been feeling."

The little man ceased, his eyes shrank back into their sockets, his figure back into its mask of shadowy brown and gleaming buttons, and Mr. Bosengate was conscious that the judge was making a series of remarks; and, very soon, of being seated at a mahogany table in the jury's withdrawing room, hearing the voice of the man with hair like an Irish terrier's saying: "Didn't he talk through his hat, that little blighter!" Conscious, too, of the commercial traveller, still on his left, always on his left! mopping his brow, and muttering: "Phew! It's hot in there to-day!" while an effluvium, as of an inside accustomed to whisky came from him. Then the man with the underlip and the three plastered wisps of hair said:

"Don't know why we withdrew, Mr. Foreman!"

Mr. Bosengate looked round to where, at the head of the table, Gentleman Fox sat, in defensive gentility and the little white piping to his waistcoat saying blandly:

"I shall be happy to take the sense of the jury."

There was a short silence, then the chemist murmured:

"I should say he must have what they call claustrophobia."

"Clauster fiddlesticks! The feller's a shirker, that's all. Missed his wife, pretty excuse! Indecent, I call it!"

The speaker was the little wire-haired man; and emotion, deep and angry, stirred in Mr. Bosengate. That ill-bred little cur! He gripped the edge of the table with both hands.

"I think it's damned natural!" he muttered. But almost before the words had left his lips he felt dismay. What had he said, he, nearly a colonel of volunteers, endorsing such a want of patriotism! And hearing the commercial traveller murmuring: "'Ear, 'ear!" he reddened violently.

The wire-headed man said roughly:

"There's too many of these blighted shirkers, and too much pampering of them."

The turmoil in Mr. Bosengate increased; he remarked in an icy voice:

"I agree to no verdict that'll send the man back to prison."

At this a real tremor seemed to go round the table, as if they all saw themselves sitting there through lunch time. Then the large grey-haired man given to winking, said:

"Oh! Come, sir, after what the judge said! Come, sir! What do you say, Mr. Foreman?"

Gentleman Fox, as who should say 'This is excellent value, but I don't wish to press it on you!' answered:

"We are only concerned with the facts. Did he or did he not try to shorten his life?"

"Of course he did, said so himself," Mr. Bosengate heard the wire-haired man snap out, and from the following murmur of assent he alone abstained. Guilty! Well, yes! There was no way out of admitting that, but his feelings revolted against handing "that poor little beggar" over to the tender mercy of his country's law. His whole soul rose in arms against agreeing with that ill-bred little cur, and the rest of this job-lot. He had an impulse to get up and walk out, saying: "Settle it your own way. Good morning."

"It seems, sir," Gentleman Fox was saying, "that we're all agreed to guilty, except yourself. If you will allow me, I don't see how you can go behind what the prisoner himself admitted."

Thus brought up to the very guns, Mr. Bosengate, red in the face, thrust his hands deep into the side pockets of his tunic, and, staring straight before him, said:

"Very well; on condition we recommend him to mercy."

"What do you say, gentlemen; shall we recommend him to mercy?"

"'Ear, 'ear!" burst from the commercial traveller, and from the chemist came the murmur:

"No harm in that."

"Well, I think there is. They shoot deserters at the front, and we let this fellow off. I'd hang the cur."

Mr. Bosengate stared at that little wire-haired brute. "Haven't you any feeling for others?" he wanted to say. "Can't you see that this poor devil suffers tortures?" But the sheer impossibility of doing this before ten other men brought a slight sweat out on his face and hands; and in agitation he smote the table a blow with his fist. The effect was instantaneous. Everybody looked at the wire-haired man, as if saying: "Yes, you've gone a bit too far there!" The "little brute" stood it for a moment, then muttered surlily:

"Well, commend 'im to mercy if you like; I don't care."

"That's right; they never pay any attention to it," said the grey-haired man, winking heartily. And Mr. Bosengate filed back with the others into court.

But when from the jury box his eyes fell once more on the hare-eyed figure in the dock, he had his worst moment yet. Why should this poor wretch suffer so, for no fault, no fault; while he, and these others, and that snapping counsel, and the Caesar-like judge up there, went off to their women and their homes, blithe as bees, and probably never thought of him again? And suddenly he was conscious of the judge's voice:

"You will go back to your regiment, and endeavour to serve your country with better spirit. You may thank the jury that you are not sent to prison, and your good fortune that you were not at the front when you tried to commit this cowardly act. You are lucky to be alive."

A policeman pulled the little soldier by the arm; his drab figure with eyes fixed and lustreless, passed down and away. From his very soul Mr. Bosengate wanted to lean out and say: "Cheer up, cheer up! I understand."

It was nearly ten o'clock that evening before he reached home, motoring back from the route march. His physical tiredness was abated, for he had partaken of a snack and a whisky and soda at the hotel; but mentally he was in a curious mood. His body felt appeased, his spirit hungry. Tonight he had a yearning, not for his wife's kisses, but for her understanding. He wanted to go to her and say: "I've learnt a lot to-day-found out things I never thought of. Life's a wonderful thing, Kate, a thing one can't live all to oneself; a thing one shares with everybody, so that when another suffers, one suffers too. It's come to me that what one has doesn't matter a bit, it's what one does, and how one sympathises with other people. It came to me in the most extraordinary vivid way, when I was on that jury, watching that poor little rat of a soldier in his trap; it's the first time I've ever felt, the—the spirit of Christ, you know. It's a wonderful thing, Kate, wonderful! We haven't been close, really close, you and I, so that we each understand what the other is feeling. It's all in that, you know; understanding, sympathy, it's priceless. When I saw that poor little devil taken down and sent back to his regiment to begin his sorrows all over again, wanting his wife, thinking and thinking of her just as you know I would be thinking and wanting you, I felt what an awful outside sort of life we lead, never telling each other what we really think and feel, never being really close. I daresay that little chap and his wife keep nothing from each other, live each other's lives. That's what we ought to do. Let's get to feeling that what really matters is, understanding and loving, and not only just saying it as we all do, those fellows on the jury, and even that poor devil of a judge, what an awful life judging one's fellow-creatures.

"When I left that poor little Tommy this morning, and ever since, I've longed to get back here quietly to you and tell you about it, and make a beginning. There's something wonderful in this, and I want you to feel it as I do, because you mean such a lot to me."

This was what he wanted to say to his wife, not touching, or kissing her, just looking into her eyes, watching them soften and glow as they surely must, catching the infection of his new ardour. And he felt unsteady, fearfully unsteady with the desire to say it all as it should be said: swiftly, quietly, with the truth and fervour of his feeling.

The hall was not lit up, for daylight still lingered under the new arrangement. He went towards the drawing-room, but from the very door shied off to his study and stood irresolute under the picture of a "Man catching a flea" (Dutch school), which had come down to him from his father. The governess would be in there with his wife! He must wait. Essential to go straight to Kathleen and pour it all out, or he would never do it. He felt as nervous as an undergraduate going up for his viva' voce. This thing was so big, so astoundingly and unexpectedly important. He was suddenly afraid of his wife, afraid of her coolness and her grace, and that something Japanese about her of all those attributes he had been accustomed to admire most; afraid, as it were, of her attraction. He felt young to-night, almost boyish; would she see that he was not really fifteen years older than herself, and she not really a part of his collection, of all the admirable appointments of his home; but a companion spirit to one who wanted a companion badly. In this agitation of his soul he could keep still no more than he could last night in the agitation of his senses; and he wandered into the dining-room. A dainty supper was set out there, sandwiches, and cake, whisky and the cigarettes, even an early peach. Mr. Bosengate looked at this peach with sorrow rather than disgust. The perfection of it was of a piece with all that had gone before this new and sudden feeling. It's delicious bloom seemed to heighten his perception of the hedge around him, that hedge of the things he so enjoyed, carefully planted and tended these many years. He passed it by uneaten, and went to the window. Out there all was darkening, the fountain, the lime tree, the flower-beds, and the fields below, with the Jersey cows who would come to your call; darkening slowly, losing form, blurring into soft blackness, vanishing, but there none the less, all there, the hedge of his possessions. He heard the door of the drawing-room open, the voices of his wife and the governess in the hall, going up to bed. If only they didn't look in here! If only! The voices ceased. He was safe now, had but to follow in a few minutes, to make sure of Kathleen alone. He turned round and stared down the length of the dark dining-room, over the rosewood table, to where in the mirror above the sideboard at the far end, his figure bathed, a stain, a mere blurred shadow; he made his way down to it along the table edge, and stood before himself as close as he could get. His throat and the roof of his mouth felt dry with nervousness; he put out his finger and touched his face in the glass. 'You're an ass!' he thought. 'Pull yourself together, and get it over. She will see; of course she will!' He swallowed, smoothed his moustache, and walked out. Going up the stairs, his heart beat painfully; but he was in for it now, and marched straight into her room. Dressed only in a loose blue wrapper, she was brushing her dark hair before the glass. Mr. Bosengate went up to her and stood there silent, looking down. The words he had thought of were like a swarm of bees buzzing in his head, yet not one would fly from between his lips. His wife went on brushing her hair under the light which shone on her polished elbows. She looked up at him from beneath one lifted eyebrow.

"Well, dear, tired?"

With a sort of vehemence the single word "No" passed out. A faint, a quizzical smile flitted over her face; she shrugged her shoulders ever so gently. That gesture, he had seen it before! And in desperate desire to make her understand, he put his hand on her lifted arm.

"Kathleen, stop, listen to me!" His fingers tightened in his agitation and eagerness to make his great discovery known. But before he could get out a word he became conscious of that cool round arm, conscious of her eyes half-closed, sliding round at him, of her half-smiling lips, of her neck under the wrapper. And he stammered:

"I want—I must—Kathleen, I—"

She lifted her shoulders again in that little shrug. "Yes, I know; all right!"

A wave of heat and shame, and of God knows what came over Mr. Bosengate; he fell on his knees and pressed his forehead to her arm; and he was silent, more silent than the grave. Nothing, nothing came from him but two long sighs. Suddenly he felt her hand stroke his cheek, compassionately, it seemed to him. She made a little movement towards him; her lips met his, and he remembered nothing but that....

In his own room Mr. Bosengate sat at his wide open window, smoking a cigarette; there was no light. Moths went past, the moon was creeping up. He sat very calm, puffing the smoke out in to the night air. Curious thing-life! Curious world! Curious forces in it, making one do the opposite of what one wished; always, always making one do the opposite, it seemed! The furtive light from that creeping moon was getting hold of things down there, stealing in among the boughs of the trees. 'There's something ironical,' he thought, 'which walks about. Things don't come off as you think they will. I meant, I tried but one doesn't change like that all of a sudden, it seems. Fact is, life's too big a thing for one! All the same, I'm not the man I was yesterday, not quite!' He closed his eyes, and in one of those flashes of vision which come when the senses are at rest, he saw himself as it were far down below, down on the floor of a street narrow as a grave, high as a mountain, a deep dark slit of a street walking down there, a black midget of a fellow, among other black midgets, his wife, and the little soldier, the judge, and those jury chaps, fantoches straight up on their tiny feet, wandering down there in that dark, infinitely tall, and narrow street. 'Too much for one!' he thought; 'Too high for one, no getting on top of it. We've got to be kind, and help one another, and not expect too much, and not think too much. That's all!' And, squeezing out his cigarette, he took six deep breaths of the night air, and got into bed.